# Keeping Secrets

Grab your pillow and join the

1. Sleeping Over
2. Camping Out
3. The Trouble with Brothers
4. Keeping Secrets

# Keeping Secrets

P. J. DENTON

Illustrated by Julia Denos

SIMON AND SCHUSTER

First published in Great Britain in 2008 by
Simon & Schuster UK Ltd
Africa House, 64-78 Kingsway, London WC2B 6AH
A CBS COMPANY

Originally published in 2008 by Aladdin Paperbacks,
An imprint of Simon & Schuster Children's Publishing Division,
New York


Book design by Karin Paprochi



This book is a work of fiction. Names, characters, places and incidents are either the product of the author's imagination or are used fictitiously. Any resemblance to actual people living or dead, events or locales is entirely coincidental.

A CIP catalogue record for this book is available
from the British Library.

ISBN: 978-1-84738-271-9

Printed and bound in Great Britain by

# 1

## The Spring Spelling Bee

Jo Sanchez took a deep breath. Her palms felt damp and warm, so she wiped them on her pants. She wondered if the other kids on the stage of the Oak Tree Elementary School auditorium were getting nervous too.

"Min Choi, you're next," Ms. Paolini, the fifth-grade English teacher, called out.

Ms. Paolini was running the Spring elling Bee. She was standing at one end of the stage, reading out the words for the students to spell.

Jo watched fourth grader Min Choi step to the microphone. Ms. Paolini smiled at Min.

"Min, your word is 'satellite,'" the teacher said.

Min slowly spelled out the word. But Jo didn't pay attention. Instead, she peered down the row of chairs on either side of her. Most of them were empty now, though all of them had been full just a short while ago. She could hardly believe it—she was the last third grader left on stage! The second-to-last one, Tammy Tandrich, had been knocked out of the spelling bee in the last round. She'd misspelled the word "achieve." Now the only people left were Jo and seven other kids. All of the others were fourth or fifth graders.

Next Jo looked out into the audienc
was hard to see anything out ther

the spotlights were shining straight at the stage. That left the rest of the auditorium in shadow. But Jo was pretty sure she could see her mother sitting a few rows back. She wished her father could be there too. But he was a doctor, and he couldn't leave his patients in the middle of the day.

Min finished spelling her word. "That's correct," Ms. Paolini told her. "Good job. Now it's Jo's turn again. Ms. Sanchez, please step forward."

Jo felt a funny, jumpy sensation in her stomach. Her friends were always teasing her because she never looked nervous, not even before a big test. She tried to tell them she still *felt* nervous sometimes. But she wasn't sure they believed her.

She brushed her shoulder-length dark hair out of her face and walked to the microphone. Then, looking over at Ms. Paolini, Jo waited for her next word.

"Whoooo! Go, Jo-Jo!" someone shouted from the audience.

The whole audience started laughing, and Jo smiled. She looked down and spotted her three best friends in the front row. All three of them had been in the spelling bee too. Each time someone got knocked out by spelling a word wrong, he or she went and sat down in the first section of the audience.

Taylor Kent was the one who'd yelled out. Taylor was very smart, but she was also very impatient. She'd sped through the spelling of the word "neighbor" without stopping to remember that it was supposed to have the letter *g* in it.

Beside Taylor, Kara Wyatt was laughing and waving to Jo. Kara wasn't a very good speller, so it was no surprise that she'd been knocked out early. She'd barely even *tried* to spell the word "geography" before giggling and giving up.

Emily McDougal was sitting on Kara's other side. Emily was looking over at Mr. Mackey, the music teacher, who was sitting at the end of their row. Emily hated causing a scene or getting in trouble, so she looked kind of nervous. A lot of things made Emily nervous. For one thing, she always got nervous when she had to stand up and talk in front of other people. Jo was pretty sure that was why Emily had messed up the word "exercise" a couple of rounds earlier. Normally, Emily was one of the best spellers in the third grade.

Mr. Mackey was laughing along with everyone else. "That's enough, Miss Kent," he called down the row.

Ms. Paolini smiled at Jo. "Now that your cheering section has settled down, let's continue," she said. "Since this is the Spring Spelling Bee, the next round will consist of words that have to do with spring. Your word is 'sprout.'"

Jo nodded and thought for a moment. She heard the word "sprout" all the time at Emily's house. Emily's mother ran an organic gardening business. This time of year, all the counters and tables at the McDougal house were filled with sprouting plants.

The trouble was, Jo wasn't sure how to

spell "sprout." It sounded like it might have a *w* in it. But that didn't seem quite right.

*It rhymes with "out,"* she thought. *So maybe it's spelled like that too.*

She took another few seconds to think about that. She didn't want to make a mistake by rushing.

"Sprout," she said at last. "S-P-R-O-U-T. Sprout?"

She held her breath, glancing over at Ms. Paolini. The teacher was smiling.

"Correct," she said. "Very good, Jo."

The audience clapped. Jo returned to the line of chairs at the back of the stage. She was relieved. That had been a hard word.

"Good job," Min whispered.

"Thanks," Jo whispered back.

It was Charles Phan's turn next. He jumped out of his chair so fast that he knocked it over. That was normal for Charles. He had a lot of energy.

"I'm ready," he yelled into the microphone. "Lay it on me, Ms. Paolini."

Everyone laughed, including Jo. Charles always made people laugh. He was one of the most hyper boys in the fourth grade. He was also one of the smartest.

Charles spelled his word, "daffodil," correctly. But the next two people got theirs wrong.

"Wow, this is a hard round," Min whispered to Jo, sounding nervous. "I hope my word is easy."

"Amy Robinson is next," Jo whispered back. "She's the smartest kid in the fifth grade. She'll probably get hers right."

Min nodded. "She won the last three spelling bees, remember?" she said. "The one in the fall this year, and both of the ones last year."

Jo's guess was correct. Amy got her word right. So did two other fifth graders, along with Min.

In the next round Jo got a word she knew—"guitar." She spelled it carefully and then sat down. Charles and Amy got their words right too. But Min and the two fifth graders got theirs wrong. That left only three people on stage—Charles, Amy, and Jo.

"It looks like we're down to our final three," Ms. Paolini said before starting the next round. "Congratulations, you three. And may the best speller win!"

Jo glanced over at the two older kids. She could hardly believe she was in the final three. Her friends might not think she ever got nervous, but she was definitely nervous now!

Amy was going first in this round. Jo watched the fifth grader walk to the microphone.

"Amy, your word is 'surgery,'" Ms. Paolini said.

Amy looked over at the teacher.

"Could you repeat that word, please?" she asked.

Even though Jo was sitting behind her, she could tell that Amy was nervous. She guessed that Amy wasn't sure how to spell her word.

Sure enough, Amy spelled it wrong. "I'm sorry, Amy," Ms. Paolini said. She spelled the word correctly, then asked Amy to come over and stand beside her.

Charles was next. He got his word wrong too.

"Your turn, Jo," Ms. Paolini said. "If you get this right, you win. If not, all three of you get to try again."

"But no pressure!" Charles called out with a laugh. He and Amy were both standing at the side of the stage near Ms. Paolini, waiting to see if Jo spelled her word correctly.

Jo stepped to the microphone. Her hands were shaking a little, and her head felt funny. What if she got her word wrong? She didn't want to look stupid.

"Ready?" Ms. Paolini asked. "Jo, your word is 'choir.'"

Jo smiled. Suddenly, she felt much less nervous. It was a pretty hard word to spell, but not for her. She was a member of her church choir—she definitely knew how to spell that word!

"Choir," she said confidently. "C-H-O-I-R."

She paused for a moment to think it over once more before making it official. She definitely didn't want to make a stupid mistake.

"Choir," she finished at last.

Ms. Paolini smiled. "Correct!" she said. "We have a winner!"

# 2

## A Surprising Prize

"Way to go, Jo!" Kara cheered loudly as Jo stepped down from the stage. Kara even did a little jump and kick, just like the real cheerleaders at the high school football games. Her wavy red hair bounced around her face, falling over her eyes.

Emily and Taylor rushed forward to hug Jo. They both looked just as excited as Kara.

"That was so awesome!" Taylor exclaimed, her greenish gold eyes sparkling. "You

looked as cool as a cucumber up there. We should start calling you Super Jo!"

Emily giggled. "Super Jo, the super speller," she said.

"Thanks, guys." Jo could hardly believe she'd just won the Spring Spelling Bee. She'd beaten all those fourth and fifth graders—even Amy Robinson!

It made her feel good but also a little bashful. She was used to getting praise and attention from teachers because of her good grades. But this was different. It seemed as if the whole school was staring at her and cheering.

"Hey, Jo," someone called. "Congratulations."

Jo turned and saw that it was Amy Robinson. The older girl was smiling at her.

"Thanks." Jo felt more bashful than ever now. Fifth graders like Amy hardly ever talked to third graders. "You did really well too."

"Thanks. Well, I'd better go." Amy waved and hurried away toward her fifth-grade friends.

Kara watched her go. "Wow," she joked. "We'd better watch out. Now that Jo is friends with fifth graders, she probably won't want to hang out with us boring old third graders anymore."

"No way!" Jo said immediately. "I would never abandon the Pyjama Gang."

The Pyjama Gang was a club the four of

them—Jo, Emily, Kara, and Taylor—had formed the previous spring. Whenever they could, they all got together and had sleepover parties at one of their houses.

Taylor clapped her hands. "That gives me a great idea," she said. "Why don't we have a sleepover to celebrate your big win? We haven't had one in a while."

Emily nodded. "I could ask my parents if we could do another campout in our tent."

Kara wrapped her freckled arms around herself and pretended to shiver. "A camp-out?" she said. "I know it's spring, but it's still way too cold out for camping. Maybe I can have it at my house instead. We can lock my brothers in the basement so they won't bug us."

Just then Jo's mother rushed over, smiling proudly. *"Buen hecho,* Jo!" she cried. Her dark brown eyes, which looked just like Jo's, were dancing with excitement.

"Thanks, Mom," Jo said. She looked at her friends. "She just said 'well done.'" When her mother got excited, she sometimes forgot that not everyone could understand Spanish. Jo's whole family spoke both Spanish and English.

*"Gracias,"* Taylor said. She didn't really speak Spanish. But she'd learned how to say a few Spanish words, such as the one that meant "thank you," from her housekeeper.

Jo's mother squeezed Jo tightly. "Ready to head home?" she asked. "I can't wait to call your father and tell him about this."

The spelling bee had taken place during the last period of the day. Any parents who had come to watch could take their kids home now that it was over, even if the kids normally rode the school bus, like Jo.

"Sure, I guess." Jo wanted to stay with her friends and keep talking about their next sleepover. But she could tell her mother was eager to get home. Party planning would just have to wait.

Jo's father wasn't home when they got there, but he walked in an hour and a half later while Jo was setting the table for dinner.

"I made it!" he called out, walking across the dining room and into the kitchen. He hung up his jacket on the hook near the back door, then hurried back into the dining room. "So tell me, Jo—what was your winning word?"

He already knew Jo had won the spelling bee. Mrs. Sanchez had called him at the office to tell him that, and to find out what time he'd be home for dinner.

Jo carefully set down the stack of three white china plates she was holding. "It was 'choir,'" she told her father. "I bet they didn't know that would be such an easy word for me."

"It's not an easy word," he said, reaching over to give her a hug. "You're just a very smart girl. Exactly like your old papa."

"Thanks, Daddy." Jo giggled and hugged him back. As usual he smelled like a combination of lime aftershave, soap, and rubbing alcohol. His bristly chin tickled her forehead a little. "But Mom said I got my brain from her side of the family."

"She did, did she?" Dr. Sanchez straightened up and glanced at his wife. Mrs. Sanchez was standing in the doorway polishing a handful of silverware with a rag. "Interesting, very interesting."

Mrs. Sanchez ignored his comment. "Get those shoes off, Hector," she said. "You're tracking dirt all over my clean floors. Dinner's almost ready—we're having all of Jo's favorite foods to celebrate."

"Hamburgers and baked squash, eh?" Dr. Sanchez said.

Jo shrugged. "I wanted crab cakes, too,"

she said. "But Mom didn't have time to go over to the seafood shop this afternoon."

Her father chuckled. "Sounds like a delicious meal even without the crab cakes. But I'll have to eat fast," he said. "I need to go back to the office for a little while after dinner and take care of some paperwork."

Dr. Sanchez was a partner in a busy ear, nose, and throat medical practice. He often had to work on evenings and weekends as well as during the day. Sometimes he didn't even make it home for dinner. Jo was glad he could eat dinner with them tonight.

"Everything is just about ready," Mrs. Sanchez said. "Let's eat!"

Half an hour later, Jo had just finished her last few bites of squash when the phone rang. Her mother answered in English, then immediately switched to Spanish. A moment later she handed the phone to Jo.

"It's Grandpapa Sanchez," she said. "He wants to congratulate you."

Jo smiled and took the phone. Her grandfather lived in a town about ten miles away. Jo and her parents went to visit him at least a couple of times a month. Jo's aunt and uncle lived there too, so each visit was like a family reunion.

*"Hola,"* Jo said into the phone. Grandpapa Sanchez had been born in Mexico. He spoke English pretty well, but he still spoke Spanish better.

Jo talked to her grandfather for a few minutes while her parents cleared the table. Grandpapa Sanchez wanted to hear all about the spelling bee. He asked her to tell him every word she had to spell. Luckily, Jo remembered them all. She had a very good memory.

She hung up a few minutes later. When she turned around, she saw her parents sitting at the table watching her.

"Your mother and I have been talking, *mi cara,*" Dr. Sanchez said. "We have a great idea."

"What is it?" Jo wandered over and sat down. She wondered if her parents were going to tell her they were planning to fix crab cakes for dinner that weekend. Her mother liked crab cakes almost as much as Jo did.

But what her mother said next had nothing to do with crab cakes.

"We know you've been wanting to host

one of your sleepovers with your friends," Mrs. Sanchez said.

Jo nodded. She was the only one in the Pyjama Gang who hadn't had a party at her house yet. She had asked her parents about it several times. They had never exactly said no. But they had never exactly said yes, either. Jo knew they weren't very excited about the idea of having a sleepover at their house. They were a little older than her friends' parents, and they liked their house to be clean, neat, and quiet. At least that was what they always said when Jo asked if they could get a dog.

"Well," her father went on, "in honor of your big win today, we decided you can have a slumber party here this weekend if you want to."

Jo gasped. "I definitely want to!" she cried. "Thanks, you guys!"

She was so thrilled that she felt like

doing cartwheels, like Taylor probably would, or jumping up and down and giggling, like Kara. Instead, she just gave both of her parents big hugs.

"May I be excused?" she asked. "I want to go call my friends and tell them right now."

Taylor, Kara, and Emily were just as excited as Jo was. "This is perfect!" Emily exclaimed when she heard the news. "We were just trying to figure out where to have our next party, remember? Your parents must have read our minds!"

Jo laughed. She didn't believe in mind reading. But she knew Emily liked learning about strange things like that in some of the books she was always reading for fun.

"I'd better get off the phone," she told Emily. "I want to start making a list of stuff to do. Saturday is only four days away, and there's a lot of planning to do before then!"

# 3

## Making Plans

When Jo's bus got to school the next day, she was one of the first ones off. She couldn't wait to talk to her friends about all the plans she'd made.

Taylor and Kara were waiting at the usual meeting spot outside their homeroom. They both walked to school, so they usually got there before Jo. Emily usually arrived either first or last, depending on what time her father had to get to his job as a teacher at the high school. He dropped her off on his way to work.

"Hi there, party girl," Taylor greeted Jo. "Are you totally excited about your sleep-over?"

"I know I am!" Kara said before Jo could answer. Kara always talked fast. She had four talkative brothers, so she had to be fast and loud if she wanted to be heard.

Jo reached into her backpack. "I'm definitely excited," she said. "I spent almost two hours last night making lists."

"Lists?" Taylor wrinkled her nose. "What kind of lists?"

Kara laughed. "For my first sleepover, the only list I made was how many ways my brothers would ruin the party."

Jo remembered that sleepover. Kara had been terribly worried about her brothers playing practical jokes on them. But in the end, the girls had turned the tables. They had played a big practical joke on the boys. It had ended up being a great party.

"That's not really true," she reminded Kara. "You had a list of things to do too, right? You had us make popcorn and watch DVDs and play games."

"I guess." Kara shrugged. "But I didn't write that stuff down or anything."

"Me neither." Taylor grinned and reached over to poke Jo in the shoulder. "But this is Jo Sanchez we're talking about, remember? She even organizes her sock drawer."

Jo smiled as Taylor and Kara laughed. She was used to her friends teasing her about liking things orderly and planned out. That was okay. She knew they were only joking, just as she was when she teased Taylor about being distractible or Kara about always being hungry.

"So do you want to see my plans or not?" she asked her friends. "I can always keep them secret." Now *she* was the one

teasing *them*. She knew they would want to know what she had planned for their next sleepover.

"Give it here!" Kara cried, grabbing Jo's notebook out of her hand. She flipped it open and peered at the top of the first page. "What's this?" she asked. "It looks like you crossed something out."

Jo took back the notebook and looked down at the page. "That's where I want to write the theme of the sleepover," she said.

"But I can't decide what it should be."

Just then Emily came hurrying down the hallway toward them. She dodged around some boys from their class who were kicking someone's lunch bag around like a soccer ball.

Emily made it past the boys and reached her friends. "Hi, you guys," she said in her soft voice. "Are you talking about the sleepover?"

"Of course," Taylor said. "We were just trying to think of a good theme for it."

"Do you have any ideas?" Jo asked Emily. Emily was the best of any of them at coming up with creative stuff like spooky stories or names for people's new pets. Jo figured she would probably be good at coming up with party themes too.

"Hmm, let me see." Emily dropped her backpack at her feet and leaned against the wall. Then she reached up and twisted a strand of her long, light blond hair around one finger. She always said doing that helped her think, even though it didn't make much sense to Jo. When she tried twisting her own hair around her finger, the only thing she could think about was how tangled her hair was getting.

"The first thing I thought of was having a spelling-bee theme, since that's why I get to have the sleepover in the first place," Jo said.

Kara looked worried. "No way," she said. "I don't want to spend our sleepover thinking about spelling. It's bad enough I have to think about it during school!" She shuddered. "Why do we need a theme for a sleepover, anyway? We never had one before."

"Sure we did," Emily pointed out. She was still twisting her hair thoughtfully. "Taylor's first sleepover was to celebrate the beginning of summer. That was the theme. The others all had themes too. We just didn't call them that."

"Ooh, I know!" Taylor said. "Jo's party could have a sports theme. Oh! Or how about a soccer theme? That would be cool. We could play soccer and make cookies that look like soccer balls or something."

Jo knew that Taylor loved sports, especially soccer. But Jo wasn't that interested in soccer herself.

Kara giggled. "This is supposed to be *Jo's* party, not yours, Taylor," she said. "If Jo was going to do a sports theme, it would be tennis." She glanced at Jo, suddenly looking worried again. "You're not going to make it a tennis party, are you? I'm not very good at tennis."

"I don't think so," Jo said. "I still think it should have something to do with the spelling bee."

"No, it shouldn't," Kara protested.

Suddenly Emily stood up straight and clapped her hands. "Yes, it should!" she cried.

"What?" Kara cried. "No way! I'm not spending all night spelling!"

"Hush, K," Taylor ordered. "I'm sure Emmers doesn't want to do that either. Let her finish."

"I'm not talking about a spelling theme," Emily said. "But the sleepover is partly because of the spelling bee, right? The *Spring* Spelling Bee."

Jo's eyes widened. "I get it," she said. "You think the sleepover theme should be Spring?"

"Right." Emily smiled. "Maybe something

like Welcome to Spring. Or how about Spring Has Sprung?"

"I love it!" Taylor clapped her hands. "Spring Has Sprung! That sounds like a totally fun theme."

"Definitely." Kara looked much happier now that they weren't talking about spelling anymore. "We could decorate cookies and cupcakes with spring-colored frosting, like pink and yellow . . ."

". . . and play Spring Tag," Taylor added. "It would be like TV Tag, but instead of naming TV shows, you have to name spring stuff."

"And for dinner we could eat spring foods, like fresh peas and spinach," Emily said. "I could bring them from my mom's garden."

Jo turned to a fresh page in her notebook and reached into her bag for a pencil. "I'd better start writing all this down," she said.

At that moment the school bell rang. All up and down the hallway students scrambled for the classroom doors.

"Too late," Taylor said. "Come on, we'd better get into homeroom before we're marked late."

Once she was sitting at her homeroom desk, Jo opened her notebook again. She wanted to be sure to write down all their great ideas before she forgot any of them. At the top of a new page she wrote SPRING HAS SPRUNG in big block letters. Then she started listing all the ideas her friends had suggested out in the hall.

"Hey, what are you writing?"

Jo glanced up. Max Wolfe was standing by her desk, staring down at her notebook. He leaned over to see what she was writing, but she covered her list with her arm.

"None of your beeswax," she said. Max was a big pain in the neck. He was always teasing all the girls in their class.

Max laughed. "I know," he said. "You're probably practicing your spelling. We should call you Spelly Sanchez!"

"Shut up, Max," Kara said from across the aisle. "Leave Jo alone."

Just then Randy Blevins wandered over. He was Max's best friend. "What's going on over here?" he asked Max.

"I said we should call her Spelly Sanchez. All she cares about is stupid spelling." Max pointed at Jo. "See? She's practicing her spelling in her spare time. What a nerd!"

"Spelly Sanchez! Spelly Sanchez!" Randy yelled. He was very loud. "Hey, Spelly, how do you spell 'nerd'?"

"Everyone knows how to spell that one," Taylor spoke up before Jo could answer. She sat right behind Jo in homeroom. "It's R-A-N-D-Y."

Just then the teacher came in to start

homeroom, and the boys hurried off to sit down. Emily leaned over toward Jo. She sat in front of Kara.

"Don't let those boys bother you," she whispered. "They're stupid."

"I know," Jo said with a smile. "And don't worry. I have better things to think about than them. Like our sleepover!"

# 4

## Strange Behavior

On Thursday morning Jo was excited to get to school and talk to her friends. She and her mother had made a shopping list the afternoon before. Mrs. Sanchez had even called Emily's mother to see what fresh spring vegetables she could buy from her for the party.

After her weekly clarinet lesson, Jo had worked on her list of games. Then, after dinner, she had made a list of ideas for decorations. By now she had three whole pages full of lists and notes in her notebook. She was sure her friends would love all her ideas.

Usually Jo was a very patient person. But today she barely waited for the bus to stop before she jumped out of her seat and hurried down the aisle.

"Where are you going, Spelly?" Max called out. He rode the same bus as Jo. "Are you in a hurry to get to homeroom and practice your spelling?"

Jo ignored him. She hopped down off the bus steps and walked past Randy, who was standing there waiting for Max. Then she headed straight inside.

Her friends were already at their meeting spot today. She could see them from halfway down the hall. They were standing close together. It looked like they were whispering to one another.

Jo walked faster. She didn't run, since the school principal was standing right there by the front doors. Running in the halls wasn't allowed.

"Slow down!" Principal Lewis called out loudly. For a second Jo thought the principal was talking to her, even though she wasn't running. Then she saw Max and Randy skidding past her. They were half-walking and half-running.

"Out of our way, Spelly!" Randy yelled as they rushed past and into homeroom.

Jo was almost to her friends by now.

They all looked up when they heard Randy yell. Then they stopped talking and backed away from one another.

"Hi, you guys," Jo greeted them. "What's up?"

"Nothing!" Kara said quickly. "Nothing at all. Nope, absolutely nothing."

"Ssh." Taylor nudged Kara hard with her elbow.

"Ouch!" Kara yelped.

Taylor smiled. "Sorry." Then she looked at Jo. "What she meant to say is, what's up with you?"

"Yes," Emily said, looking worried. "What's up with you today, Jo?"

Jo frowned a little. Her friends were acting kind of weird. But she didn't worry about it for long. She was too excited to share her plans.

"I wanted to show you guys my lists," she said. "The Spring Has Sprung theme gave me lots of great ideas." She smiled at

Emily. "My mom loves it too. She thinks we can get a tulip-shaped cake from the bakery. Get it? Tulips grow in the spring."

"That sounds cool," Taylor said. She looked over at Kara. "Doesn't that sound cool, Kara?"

"Totally cool," Kara agreed. Then she giggled, even though no one had said anything funny.

That was a little strange. But not *too* strange. Kara always giggled a lot. And she loved cake.

"Mom had another great idea," Jo said. "She thinks we should make a big banner to hang in the front hallway. It can have my name on it, and 'Spring Has Sprung,' and also my winning spelling-bee word."

She looked at her friends to see what they thought of the idea. Taylor was looking at Kara again. One of her eyebrows was raised, and her lips were pursed. Kara looked back at her, then covered her mouth quickly. But another giggle came out anyway.

"What's the matter?" Jo asked them. "Don't you like the banner idea?"

"We love it," Taylor answered. "Great idea. Definitely."

"Yeah," Kara added. She giggled again. "Definitely."

Jo frowned. She glanced over at Emily, who was being quiet. "What's wrong with them?" she asked.

"Who?" Emily asked.

"What do you mean, 'who?'" Jo waved one hand at Taylor and Kara. "Them. Why are they acting so weird?"

Emily shrugged. "I don't know what you mean. They always act weird." She laughed, then checked her watch. "Hey, shouldn't we go into homeroom soon? We don't want to be late."

"Let's go!" Taylor agreed. She grabbed

her backpack off the floor and scooted into the classroom. Kara and Emily were right behind her.

Jo followed more slowly. She was pretty sure she wasn't imagining things. Her friends weren't acting like their normal selves. What was going on?

The bell rang just as Jo sat down at her desk. All around her, other kids were setting down their backpacks and sliding into their seats. Her three friends all looked very busy putting their backpacks away. None of them looked over at her.

Jo looked down at her desk. She noticed several words written in pencil on its wooden surface. At least they were sort of like words. Most of them were spelled wrong. The words were SMARTY PANTZ, SPELUNG BE, and NURD.

She heard snorts of laughter from nearby. Looking up, she saw Max and Randy watching her.

"What are you reading, Spelly?" Max called.

Jo didn't answer. But this time it wasn't because she was trying to ignore the boys. This time it was because she was too upset.

She wasn't upset about the boys' silly prank. She was sure Max and Randy were the ones who had written the misspelled words on her desk. That was the kind of thing they were always doing.

But their stupid pranks didn't bother her. What bothered her was the idea that had just popped into her mind. It was a theory about why her friends were acting so weird all of a sudden.

Jo started rubbing the words off her desk with her eraser while she tried to figure out if her theory could be right. The more she thought about it, the more sense it made. After all, the boys hadn't started calling her Spelly until after the spelling bee. Just like Jo's friends hadn't started acting strangely until after the spelling bee.

Could her best friends be jealous of her big win?

# 5

## Keeping Secrets

Jo thought about her theory all morning. She tried to figure out if it could be true. She thought about how smart Emily was, and how well she always did in school. It was probably hard for her to watch Jo win, when she was just as good a speller.

Then there was Taylor. Taylor loved to win. She hated when anyone beat her at soccer or running or most other sports.

Maybe she hated losing the spelling bee too. Even to one of her best friends.

Kara probably didn't care at all about not winning the spelling bee. But she was the type of person who got excited when other people were excited, and sad when her friends were sad. Maybe she got jealous when others were jealous too.

*Yes,* Jo thought as she sat in math class. *I think this could explain why they're acting so weird.*

She decided to talk to her friends at lunchtime. There was no point in trying to ignore the bad feelings. They needed to talk about what was bothering them right away so they could go back to planning their sleepover.

Jo waited until the four of them were sitting at their regular table in the corner of the cafeteria. Then she took a deep breath.

"Listen, you guys," she said. "Are you upset about the spelling bee?"

Taylor looked up from unwrapping her sandwich. "What are you talking about?"

"I'm talking about this morning. You three were acting weird." Jo looked straight at Taylor, then turned to look at the other two too. Kara stared back at her, her big hazel eyes looking confused. Emily was gazing down at her lunch with her long, straight blond hair hiding half of her face.

"Weird?" Kara said. "What do you mean? We weren't acting weird."

"Yes, you were," Jo said. "But it's okay. I think I figured out why. You're upset because I won the spelling bee and you didn't."

Taylor laughed. "What?" she exclaimed. "No way. We're totally proud of you, Jo-Jo!"

"Yeah." Kara giggled. "What makes you think I even want to win a spelling bee? For one thing, if I did, everyone I know would probably pass out from the shock."

She sat up a little straighter. "Hey, that includes my brothers. Maybe next time I *should* try to win."

Emily reached over and squeezed Jo's hand. "We're all happy for you, Jo," she said. "Really."

Jo could tell she meant it. Emily wasn't a very good liar. Whenever she tried to lie, her lips quivered and her expression got all funny. She was pretty sure Taylor was telling the truth about not being upset too. When Taylor was really upset about losing a soccer game or something, she stomped around and acted grumpy.

"Okay," Jo said. "So then why were you all acting like weirdos this morning?"

"We weren't," Kara said quickly. "You must have been imagining it."

"Or if we were," Taylor put in, "it was probably because, um, right before you got there, Randy and his stupid friends were goofing off and acting like jerks."

"Yeah!" Kara's face lit up. "That's probably it. You know what jerks they can be. We were just, like, upset or something. Probably."

Emily didn't say anything. She suddenly seemed very busy sticking her straw into her juice box. Her hair was hanging over her face again.

"Oh." Jo wasn't sure what else to say. She could tell her friends weren't telling her the truth now. The trouble was, she wasn't sure what to do about it. She'd never had that sort of problem with her best friends before. Usually they told one another everything.

*Well, not always,* she thought as her friends started talking about something else. *There was the time Taylor didn't tell us she was afraid of spiders. And the time Kara didn't tell us her brothers were making her be their servant.*

Then she shook her head. Neither of those times were the same sort of thing. For one thing, neither of those secrets had stayed secret for very long. Besides, both of those times it had been one of them keeping secrets from the other three. This time it was all three of the others keeping a secret from her.

Jo didn't cry very often, but she felt a little like crying now. What could her friends be keeping from her? Why wouldn't they tell her the truth?

For the rest of the day Jo couldn't stop thinking about her problem. No matter how hard she thought about it, she couldn't figure out what was wrong.

There was only one thing to do. She had to try talking to them again. She decided she would do it after school. Usually they all hung out together for a few minutes before Jo had to get on her bus and Emily went to meet her dad.

After the final bell rang, they all wandered out toward their usual spot near the front doors. "Hey, you guys," Jo said. "I want to talk to you about something."

"Sorry, Jo-Jo," Taylor said. She looked at her watch. "It will have to wait until tomorrow. I have an early soccer match tonight, so I need to hurry home."

"Me too," Kara said. She giggled. "Um, I mean, not about the soccer match. But I need to get home early to, um . . ."

Taylor elbowed her. "You told me you have to rush home to feed your neighbor's cat," she said. "Remember?"

"Oh, right." Kara giggled. "He's always hungry."

"I told my dad I'd wait for him out front today," Emily added softly. "I think he's in a hurry too."

"Oh." Jo shrugged. "Well, I guess I might as well go get right on my bus, then. See you tomorrow."

"Bye!" her friends called as they hurried off. "See you tomorrow, Jo!"

Jo sighed as she watched them go. Then she went and got on her bus. Almost none of the other kids were there yet, so she sat down in a seat by herself near the front. She pulled out her notebook and opened it on her lap to her party-planning page. The list of party decorations was almost finished, though she still needed to work on the list of spring-themed games and activities.

But she couldn't concentrate on that.

Her mind kept returning to her friends and their weird behavior.

*I know,* she thought as she stared down at her lists. *Maybe I should make a list for this problem too.*

She got out a pencil and turned to a blank page. At the top she wrote BEST FRIENDS ACTING WEIRD. Then under that she wrote THEORIES.

Then she wrote #1: JEALOUS ABOUT SPELLING BEE.

She thought about their talk at lunch. She tried to remember everything the others had said. The more she thought about it, the more certain she was that theory #1 was wrong. So she crossed it off.

Next she wrote down a few more theories: THEY DON'T LIKE ME ANYMORE and I'M IMAGINING IT ALL and FRIENDS IN BAD MOOD TODAY. She thought about those for a while, but she wasn't sure they made sense. She even wrote down FRIENDS TAKEN OVER

BY ALIENS. That one made her laugh. It sounded like something Emily or Kara would think up. She crossed it off the list right away.

Then she sighed and looked around. A few other kids were climbing onto the bus by now. Max hopped on board with another boy. When he passed her seat, he stuck out his tongue at her.

"What're you doing, Spelly?" he asked. "Are you trying to write down every spelling word there is?"

The other boy, a second grader named Robby, laughed loudly. "Yeah, school's over, Spelly!" he cried. "You can stop writing stuff down now."

Jo ignored them as they pushed and shoved each other toward the back of the bus. They had just given her an idea for another theory, and this one made a lot more sense than any of the others. . . .

# 6

## A Dramatic Moment

As soon as Jo entered the school building on Friday morning, she spotted her friends. The three of them were in their usual spot. Once again they were leaning close together, whispering to one another.

Jo didn't hesitate. This time she was sure she'd figured out why they were acting so weird. And she was ready to do something about it.

She marched down the hall. "Hi," she said.

The three of them stopped whispering immediately. "Oh hi, Jo," Kara said. "And bye, Jo. I was just about to run to the bathroom."

"I need to leave too," Emily said. "I have to go get a book from the library before homeroom."

"Wait!" Jo said before they could move. "Don't go anywhere. I need to talk to you about something important."

Taylor bit her lip and glanced at Kara and Emily. "Really?" she said. "Um, can it wait till lunchtime? Because I need to—"

"No!" Jo said, not even letting her finish. "I've been thinking about it all night, and it can't wait. Especially since the sleepover is tomorrow."

"Oh." Kara shrugged, looking sort of nervous. "Um, okay. What?"

Jo took a deep breath. She knew what she had to do. Reaching into her backpack, she pulled out her notebook.

"Are you showing us your lists again?" Taylor asked, wrinkling her forehead.

Jo didn't answer. She opened her notebook to the pages of party plans. Then she ripped them out.

"Why did you do that?" Kara asked.

"I'm doing what you guys want," Jo said. She hesitated for only a second, looking down at her neatly printed lists. Then she ripped the pages right in half.

Emily gasped. "What are you doing, Jo? Those are your sleepover lists!"

"This doesn't mean the party is canceled, does it?" Kara cried.

"Nothing like that, don't worry," Jo said. "I just wanted to show you that I realized what was wrong."

"What was wrong with what?" Taylor looked confused as she stared from Jo to the ripped pages and back again.

"With my party plans." Jo waved the pages in the air. "I finally figured out why you guys were acting so weird. I've been treating this sleepover like a school project or something instead of a party." She shrugged. "I know you guys aren't like that. That's why you keep teasing me about my lists. You wish we could have a regular, less planned, more relaxed type of sleepover, like usual. So that's what I'm going to do."

All three of them just stared at her for a few seconds. Even Kara was silent for once.

Emily was the first one to smile, then giggle. "Oh, Jo!" she exclaimed, reaching out to touch the ripped pages. "I can't believe you just did that. Ripping up your lists was . . . was . . . well, it was like something *Kara* would do!"

Kara started to giggle too. "Yeah," she agreed. "I must be rubbing off on you, Jo."

"Maybe you're rubbing off on her a little," Taylor said. "But she's still our Jo-Jo. Otherwise she wouldn't even have all those lists to rip up!"

“True,” Emily said. “But don’t worry, Jo. We like you that way—honest!”

Kara nodded. “We’re looking forward to our totally planned and organized sleepover.”

“We’d expect nothing less from you,” Taylor put in with a grin.

Jo blinked in surprise. She stared at Taylor, then at Kara, then at Emily. All three of them were smiling or laughing. Finally Jo smiled too.

“Really?” she asked. “So you weren’t annoyed with all my lists?”

“No way,” Taylor said. The others shook their heads too.

Jo was relieved. She was willing to have whatever kind of sleepover her friends wanted. But it had felt terrible to think that they didn’t like the way she was planning it. After all, she was just being herself. She liked to be organized and make lists. It was a part of her personality, just the way liking sports was part of Taylor's, loving animals and books was part of Emily's, and being talkative was part of Kara's.

"I still can't believe you ripped up your lists," Kara said.

"We can help you rewrite them at lunch if you want," Emily offered.

Jo smiled. "That's okay," she said, tucking the ripped pages into her backpack. "I have the whole thing saved on my computer at home."

The others all laughed. "That's our Jo!" Taylor cried just as the bell rang to summon them into homeroom.

"Come on," Emily said, grabbing her backpack and slinging it over one shoulder. "We'd better go in."

Kara was still giggling. "Ripping up that list was definitely the biggest surprise of the week," she said. "Unless there's an even *bigger* surprise coming at the sleepover."

"No way," Taylor said instantly. "This is Jo we're talking about, remember? She plans everything—no surprises."

Jo was already turning to head into the classroom. She paused and glanced over her shoulder to add a joke of her own.

But she bit back the words. She was just in time to see Taylor poking Kara in the arm. Kara was grinning back at Taylor, rolling her eyes. Emily was chewing her lower lip and staring anxiously at both of them.

Jo's heart sank. She was glad that her friends weren't upset about her lists and plans. But she realized she still had no idea what their secret really was.

# 7

## A New Plan

"Excuse me, you guys," Taylor said, pushing back from her seat at the lunch table. "I need to go to the bathroom."

"Okay," Kara said.

Taylor leaned over her. "Don't you need to go too, K?" she asked.

Kara quickly swallowed the bite of chocolate-chip cookie she was chewing. "Oops!" she said. "I forgot. Um, I mean, yes. I do have to go."

She hopped up from her seat. Then she

and Taylor hurried off across the cafeteria toward the restrooms.

Jo narrowed her eyes and watched them go. "What was that all about?" she said.

"What?" Emily seemed to be very busy rearranging the lettuce on her sandwich. She didn't look up at Jo.

Jo sighed. "Never mind."

❊ ❊ ❊

All day it was the same thing. Every time Jo convinced herself there was nothing going on, she caught her friends whispering or trading funny looks or doing something else that made her think there *was* something going on. But what was she supposed to do? She'd asked them about it several times already. If they didn't want to tell her, she couldn't make them.

After school Jo had to stay behind for a few minutes to ask the teacher a question. When she stepped outside, she saw her friends whispering together. As soon as she joined them, they all found reasons to rush away.

"See you tomorrow, Jo-Jo," Taylor said as she hurried off.

"Yeah," Kara called back over her shoulder. "We can't wait for the sleepover!"

Emily giggled, then bit her lip. "Um, bye," she said. Then she scooted away toward the parent pick-up area.

Jo stood there alone for a moment before walking slowly toward her bus. Suddenly, she wasn't looking forward to her sleepover at all. What if her friends acted this way all through it? If they did, it wasn't likely to be much fun at all.

*The best thing about the Pyjama Gang is hanging out with my best friends,* she thought. *But right now they're not acting much like friends at all.*

She stopped short, struck by a terrible thought. Max Wolfe was walking right behind her. He bumped into her.

"Hey!" he said. "Watch where I'm going, Spelly."

He hurried around her and raced toward the bus. She didn't move, or even notice him. She was too busy worrying over her terrible thought.

What if her friends didn't want to be best friends with her anymore?

She shook her head, not believing it

could be true. The four of them had been best friends since kindergarten. They would always be friends. Wouldn't they?

Just then the bus engine started up with a roar. Jo began walking again. Her feet automatically took her to the right bus, up the steps, and down the aisle to an empty seat. But her brain wasn't paying attention to where she was going. She was too busy trying to figure out whether her horrible idea could be true.

Jo felt a little bit better when she climbed out of the car at the tennis club. She loved everything about her tennis lessons. She loved the neat, clean white skirt, top, and sneakers she wore. She loved the fancy red and silver racket her aunt and uncle had given her for her last birthday. She loved figuring out how to hit the ball at exactly the right angle to skim over the net. She loved the weird way tennis players kept score—not zero-one-two-three like most sports, but love-fifteen-thirty-forty. And she loved the five other kids in her lesson. All of them except for one went to Birch Bark Elementary on the west side of town, so the only time she got to see them was at tennis.

"Hi, Jo!" Maureen Caldwell called when Jo hopped out of her mother's car. "What's up?"

"Nothing," Jo said, even though that wasn't really true. It would just be too complicated to explain what had been worrying her all day.

Marie Torelli laughed. She was the only other kid in the lesson who went to Oak Tree Elementary with Jo. "Jo's just being modest," Marie said, swinging her racket back and forth. "She won our school spelling bee this week. She beat all the fourth and fifth graders!"

"Wow, that's cool, Jo." Lanie Miller

smiled at her. "Congratulations. I was in our spelling bee last month, but I messed up on the very first word. Totally embarrassing!"

Jo giggled. "What word was it?"

Lanie rolled her eyes. "I can't even remember. I think I might have fainted after that."

That made all of them laugh. Lanie was one of those people who was really funny even when she wasn't saying anything that silly. It made her a great person to be around.

The other girls continued to talk and laugh. But Jo wasn't paying attention anymore. She'd just had a great idea.

*Maybe I should invite a few extra people to my sleepover,* she thought. *Just in case.*

She looked around at her tennis friends. All of them were nice and lots of fun. Jo had been to birthday parties at several of their houses, and she always had a good time.

If Marie and Lanie and the others came to her party, it wouldn't matter what Jo's best friends did—even if they decided not to show up at all. Jo knew it wasn't very likely that her best friends wouldn't come to the sleepover. But she wasn't sure how likely it was that they would be acting normal again by then.

Jo smiled. It was the perfect plan. She knew she should check with her parents first, but there was no time for that. It was already Friday afternoon, and the sleepover was tomorrow. She was sure her parents would understand.

"Hey," she blurted out, right in the middle of a funny story Lanie was telling about her older sister. "Do you guys want to come to my sleepover?"

# 8

## Phone Frustration

Lanie was the first one to answer. "A sleepover?" she said. "That sounds like a blast. But I already have plans on Saturday. Sorry!"

"That's okay." Suddenly, Jo thought of something. "Hey, how did you know it was Saturday? I didn't tell you that yet."

Lanie laughed and tapped her tennis racket against her leg. "Oh, yeah," she said. "Well, sleepovers are always on Saturday, right?"

"They could be on Friday," Marie pointed out. Then she smiled at Jo. "Sorry," she said. "I wish I could go. But I'm visiting my grandparents this weekend."

The other girls spoke up too. It turned out that all of them already had plans for Saturday night.

"No problem," Jo said. She was disappointed, but not that surprised. After all, she hadn't given them much notice. A lot of kids had things to do on the weekends.

Besides, her tennis friends weren't her only other friends. . . .

As soon as she got home from her lesson, Jo went to the phone in the two-story front foyer. Her mother kept a little green notebook beside the phone, where she wrote down the numbers of everyone she called. Jo flipped through it to the section labeled CHURCH PEOPLE.

She smiled as she dialed the first number. Her choir friends were just as much fun as her tennis friends. She was sure some of them would want to come to her sleepover.

By the time she hung up a half hour later, her smile had disappeared.

"This is crazy," she muttered as she checked the list once more to be sure she hadn't skipped anyone. She hadn't. She had called every one of her choir friends. And none of them could come to her party either!

Jo wasn't sure what to do next. She thought about calling her older sister and brother for advice. But they were both off at college in another state. She wasn't supposed to call them from the regular phone—only from her father's cell phone, which had free long-distance minutes.

She set the phone down and stared at it. What was going on? She was starting to wonder if she had any real friends at all. A few of her choir friends had sounded weird when she'd invited them—like they weren't sure what to say at first. But in the end, all of them had said no.

Then she thought back to her tennis friends. A few of their answers had been a little strange too. Like Lanie saying she was busy before she even knew for sure when the sleepover was going to be.

Jo was confused by it all. What in the world was wrong with everyone? Why didn't anybody want to come to her sleepover? Even her best friends didn't seem that excited about it. In fact, Jo wasn't sure she was that excited about it herself anymore. Maybe it would be better if she canceled the whole thing.

She wandered across the foyer and into

her mother's home office. That was where Mrs. Sanchez ran her business. She went to yard sales and thrift shops and bought china and knickknacks. Then she sold them for a higher price on the Internet. Today she was busy wrapping up a pretty rose-colored plate in tissue paper.

Mrs. Sanchez smiled when she saw Jo. "There you are, Jo," she said. She set down the plate and brushed off her hands on her pants. "I was just going to come see if you want to help me get dinner ready. Your father should be home any minute now."

"Sure." Jo trailed after her mother down the hall and into the spacious, green-tiled kitchen. She could smell chicken baking in the oven. "Listen, Mom. About the sleepover . . ."

"Don't worry," Mrs. Sanchez said before Jo could finish. "I finished most of the shopping today. I'll just need to run out in the morning for a few last-minute things. Then I can help you with the banner and the other decorations."

Jo didn't get a chance to answer. At that moment her father came in shouting hello. Soon all three of them were sitting down to eat.

"How was your day, *mi cara*?" Dr. Sanchez asked Jo as he helped himself to some peas and carrots. "Do anything fun at school?"

"Just the usual." Jo was distracted. She stirred the vegetables on her plate, trying to figure out how to tell her parents she didn't want to have the sleepover after all. They had already made so many plans. She was afraid to just come out and say it.

"Are your friends getting excited about the party?" her father asked cheerfully.

"Sure, I guess." Jo cleared her throat, suddenly getting an idea. The reason her parents hadn't wanted her to host a sleepover for so long was because they didn't want their house messed up. If Jo reminded them how messy her friends could be, maybe they would decide to cancel the party themselves. "Um, Kara says she's probably going to be extra hungry tomorrow," she said. "I just hope she doesn't laugh with her mouth full. The last time she did that, she dribbled tomato sauce all over the floor."

Her mother chuckled. "Oh, dear," she said. "Maybe I'd better pick up some extra carpet cleaner while I'm out tomorrow."

"That Kara is a character," Dr. Sanchez said. "Things are never boring when she's around, that's for sure."

Jo decided to try again. "I already told Taylor she's not allowed to play soccer in the house," she said. "I just hope she remembers. You know how hyper she is sometimes." She glanced around. "Mom, maybe you'd better put away your vases and figurines and all the rest of the breakable stuff around here."

"Don't worry, Jo." Mrs. Sanchez reached for the platter of chicken. "We'll take away her soccer ball when she comes in. That should keep my things safe."

"That reminds me," Dr. Sanchez said. "On my way home I passed a sign for a spring carnival at the community center. How about if I take you and your friends over there to start off your sleepover? The sign said they're having a soccer ball-kicking contest." He laughed. "Maybe we can wear out Taylor before she gets here."

"Sure, that sounds fine." Jo tried to sound excited about her father's suggestion. But she was glad when her mother changed the subject to something else.

After dinner Jo decided to try once more to figure out what was going on with her friends. She asked if she could use the phone to call them.

She tried Taylor's house first. Mr. Kent

answered and told her that Taylor was still at her soccer match.

Next Jo dialed Emily's number. But the line was busy. So was Kara's.

Kara's line was almost always busy. Her brothers liked to play online video games for hours at a time. But Emily's family didn't spend very much time on the phone.

*That means Kara and Em are probably talking to each other,* Jo thought as she set down the phone. *Probably about whatever they've been whispering about all week.*

She looked at the clock on the wall, trying to figure out how many hours, minutes, and seconds were left until the sleepover started. But it wasn't because she was excited—just the opposite. So far, this was shaping up to be the worst sleepover ever.

# 9

## Spelling Things Out

"Come on, Taylor!" Kara cried, clapping her hands. "Try again!"

"You can do it," Emily added.

Jo smiled as Taylor made a face. It was Saturday afternoon, and the four of them were at the spring carnival with Jo's father. So far, things seemed to be back to normal. But Jo still hadn't forgotten about her friends' weird behavior all week.

"Okay, I'll try one more time. But then I'm out of quarters." Taylor fished some change out of her pocket. She was playing the soccer ball–kicking game at the carnival. So far she had won two stuffed animals and a baseball cap. But she couldn't seem to win the giant stuffed panda she wanted.

"Hurry up and win, Taylor." Kara licked her lips. "Jo's dad promised us ice cream on the way home, remember?"

Emily looked at her watch. "Don't worry," she said. "We have plenty of time before we have to be back." She shot Jo a glance. "For the sleepover, I mean."

Kara giggled. "We know *exactly* what you mean, Em."

Jo frowned a little. Was it her imagination, or were her three friends trading a very strange look right now?

*I always thought Kara and Emily were the super sensitive ones,* she thought. *Not me. I must be going crazy.*

Taylor didn't win on her next kick. But Dr. Sanchez gave her some more quarters, and finally she won the panda. "Whoo-hoo!" she cried as the game worker handed her the huge stuffed animal. "Isn't he cool? I think I'll call him Peter. Get it? Peter Panda!"

"I just hope we can fit him in the car," Jo commented. "I still don't see why we couldn't drop off the sleeping bags and stuff at home before we came."

"Waste of time," her father said. "We didn't want to miss anything here. Right, girls?"

"Right." Kara giggled. "We're on a schedule."

Taylor and Emily giggled too. But Jo just frowned. She didn't see what was so funny. And she still didn't understand why they couldn't have dropped off her friends' things after her father picked them up. All those suitcases and sleeping bags made the car awfully crowded.

She forgot about that for a while once

they made it to the ice cream parlor. Her father bought them all cones with any two flavors they wanted, and for a little while the four girls laughed and kidded around with one another just like always. Jo started to wonder if she really was just imagining that something was wrong.

After they finished their cones, the girls all crowded back into the car. Jo sat in the front seat beside her father, with Peter Panda crammed in between them. The other three girls were in the back.

For the first few miles everyone talked about the carnival and the ice cream they'd just eaten. Then, after a while, there were a few minutes of silence.

*The ice cream parlor was fun,* Jo thought. *Maybe this sleepover really will turn out fine after all. . . .*

Pushing Peter Panda's big fuzzy head aside, she glanced back at her friends. She was just in time to see Emily lean over something in her lap. Then Emily scribbled something on it with a pencil she was holding.

For a moment Jo was confused. Then she saw Emily pass the thing she was holding to Taylor. It was a piece of paper. They were writing notes to one another!

Jo gasped. "Okay, that's enough!" she cried, suddenly feeling fed up with the whole situation. "What are you writing? What's going on?"

Three sets of startled eyes stared at her. Taylor's greenish gold eyes looked startled. Emily's blue ones looked worried. And Kara's hazel ones formed perfect round circles as she stared at Jo.

The first person to answer was Dr. Sanchez. "Here's your answer, Jo," he said with a chuckle. "Look—we're home."

Jo hadn't even noticed that they had reached her subdivision. She looked out the window as the car pulled into her driveway, and her eyes widened to match her friends'.

"Oh my gosh!" she cried.

Hanging over the front door was a big banner. Red letters spelled out CONGRATULATIONS, JO! Just below that was the banner she and her mother had made featuring her winning spelling-bee word. People were pouring out of the house and

waving. She spotted her mother, her aunt and uncle, and Grandpapa Sanchez. Right behind them were her older brother and sister. She also saw some of her neighbors, kids from school, and all sorts of other familiar faces.

"Whew!" Kara cried from the backseat, clapping her hands. "I'm glad we're here. I couldn't keep that secret for one second longer!"

Taylor laughed. "Yeah," she said. "I think Jo-Jo was about to beat us up to get us to tell."

"Surprise!" Emily exclaimed. "It's a party to celebrate you winning the spelling bee, Jo!"

For a moment Jo couldn't speak. Her cheeks grew hot as she remembered how angry she'd been with her friends. She should have known they wouldn't keep secrets from her without a very good reason!

"Look," she exclaimed. "There are Lanie and Maureen from tennis."

Her father nodded as he turned off the car. "Your pals from choir are here too," he said.

"So that's why none of them said they'd come," Jo murmured to herself. "They didn't want to give away the surprise."

"What was that, *mi cara*?" her father asked.

Jo shook her head. "Never mind," she said. She waved to her brother and sister. "I can't believe Lydia and Al are here!"

"They didn't want to miss it," her father said. "They both came home from college last night and stayed over with friends so you wouldn't know they were here. We wanted this whole thing to be a big surprise."

"Don't worry, it was," Jo said. "Come on, let's go say hi to everyone."

She spent the next half hour talking to the party guests. It seemed as if everyone wanted to hear her spell her winning word. Jo must have spelled "choir" at least two dozen times.

Finally, she met up with her three best friends in the kitchen. They had all just helped themselves to sodas.

"So did you like the surprise?" Emily asked Jo, sounding a little worried. "We weren't sure you would."

Jo smiled at her. "I love it," she said. "But I can't believe I didn't guess what was going on! You guys aren't very good at keeping secrets, you know."

Taylor laughed. "Yeah," she said. "Kara's the worst."

"Hey! I'm not the one who almost gave it away at the carnival," Kara protested. "That was you, Em."

Emily giggled. "I guess we're lucky a super smarty like Jo didn't figure it out," she said. "She must have been too busy making lists for the sleepover."

Jo smiled. She didn't tell them how worried she had been all week. It didn't matter. The important thing was that everything had turned out just fine in the end.

"Hey, that reminds me," she said. "Are you guys still staying over tonight after everybody else leaves?"

"Of course!" Kara replied. "Even I know how to spell our favorite word: s-l-e-e-p-o-v-e-r!"

# Slumber Party Project: Fun and Games

Looking for some cool games to play at your next sleepover? Try one of these party classics.

WHISPER DOWN THE LANE: Everyone sits in a long row. The first person in line whispers a sentence to the next person. (Hint: Something a little bit long and complicated makes things more fun.) Then each person whispers the sentence they hear to the next person in line. But they can only say it once—no repeats. When the sentence reaches the far end, that person says what they heard out loud. Chances are it won't sound like the same sentence at all!

TV TAG: This is a variety of Freeze Tag. When the person who is "it" tags someone, that person must freeze in place. Anyone else can unfreeze that person by tagging them while yelling out the name of a TV show. Each show name can only be used once per game. (You can also try Movie Tag, Book Tag, Animal Tag, or any other category you can invent.)

MOTHER MAY I?: One person is "Mother." Everyone else stands in a line facing her. Mother then picks someone and gives her an order. For example: "Jump up and down three times" or "Touch your toes." That person must ask, "Mother May I?" before performing the task. If she forgets and just goes ahead and does it, she's out. If she does it right, Mother picks someone else and gives her a different order. Again, the person must ask, "Mother May I?" before following the order. (This game is harder than it sounds!) The last person left is the winner and gets to be Mother for the next round.